WHAT SHOULD A HORSE SAY?

For Rochelle and Hayden who inspired me to write. FM

For speech therapists, particularly Jackson. AW

WHAT SHOULD A HORSE SAY?

Fleur McDonald
Illustrated by Annie White

Farmer Rochelle owned a cow who said moo moo,
a sheep who said baa baa
and a horse who said ... chick chick!

Farmer Hayden came to visit on his quad bike.

He was carrying a cardboard box.

Farmer Rochelle looked in the box. Inside were six baby chickens saying:

chick chick, chick chick!

'Wow,' said Farmer Rochelle in surprise.
'My cow says moo moo,
my sheep says baa baa,
my chickens say chick chick
AND my horse says chick chick!
Farmer Hayden, what should a horse say?'

'I'm not sure,' said Farmer Hayden. 'My tractor says brum brum,
my quad bike says broom broom
and my truck says clatter clatter clunk.
I don't know what a horse should say.'

Farmer Rochelle had to find out. She rang her friend Susan.

'Susan, I have a cow who says moo moo,

a sheep who says baa baa,

chickens who say chick chick

AND a horse who says chick chick.

What should a horse say?'

'I'm not sure, Farmer Rochelle.
I have a dog who says woof woof,
a cat who says meow meow
and a cocky who says:

Can I have
more chocolate?
Squark!

I don't know what a horse should say.'

Farmer Rochelle spoke to another friend

and another friend

and ANOTHER friend,

but no-one knew what a horse should say.

'I think we need a vet,' said Farmer Hayden.

Dr Swan the vet came to visit.

'Dr Swan,' said Rochelle,
'I own a cow who says moo moo,
a sheep who says baa baa,
chickens who say chick chick
AND a horse who says chick chick.
What should a horse say?'

'Hmm,' said Dr Swan. He patted the horse and looked into his dark brown eyes. 'Nothing wrong there.'

Dr Swan looked in his ears with a torch. 'Nothing wrong there.'

'Beep,' went the thermometer as Dr Swan took the horse's temperature. 'Nothing wrong there.'

'Hmm,' he said again as he looked down the horse's throat.
'Oh! Uh-huh. I see. He has a problem with his voice box.'

Dr Swan gave the horse some
funny-tasting medicine …

… and rubbed some bright yellow cream on his throat.

Then he took some oats out of his bag.

The horse sniffed them and then started to eat.

When he had finished, the horse
looked up and said …

NEIGH NEIGH!

'That's what a horse should say!'